Brilliant Plot

VIOLET MACKEREL'S

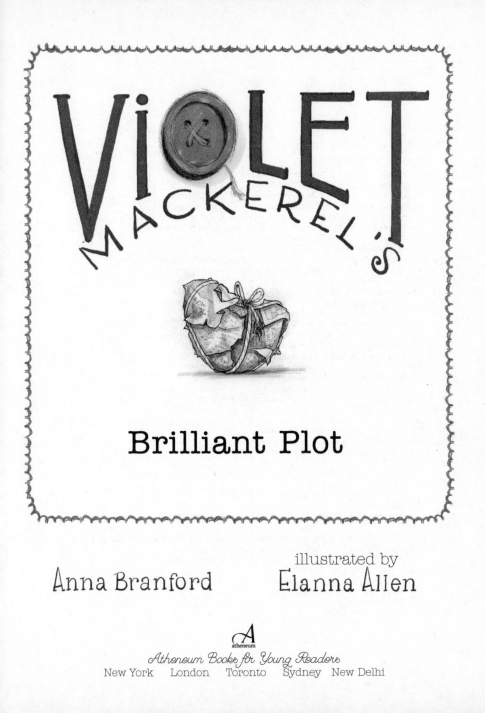

Brilliant Plot

Anna Branford

illustrated by Elanna Allen

Atheneum Books for Young Readers
New York   London   Toronto   Sydney   New Delhi

$\mathcal{A}$
atheneum

Atheneum Books For Young Readers

An imprint of Simon & Schuster Children's Publishing Division
1230 Avenue of the Americas, New York, New York 10020

Text copyright © 2010 by Anna Branford
Illustrations copyright © 2012 by Elanna Allen
Text was originally published in 2010 by Walker Books Australia Pty Ltd.

ATHENEUM BOOKS FOR YOUNG READERS is a registered trademark of
Simon & Schuster, Inc.
Atheneum logo is a trademark of Simon & Schuster, Inc.
For information about special discounts for bulk purchases,
please contact Simon & Schuster Special Sales at 1-866-506-1949
or business@simonandschuster.com.
The Simon & Schuster Speakers Bureau can bring authors to your
live event. For more information or to book an event, contact the
Simon & Schuster Speakers Bureau at 1-866-248-3049 or visit our
website at www.simonspeakers.com.
Also available in an Atheneum Books for Young Readers
hardcover edition.
Book design by Lauren Rille
The text for this book is set in Excelsior.
The illustrations for this book are rendered in pencil with digital ink.
Manufactured in the United States of America
0318 MTN

10 9 8
Library of Congress Cataloging-in-Publication Data
Branford, Anna.
Violet Mackerel's brilliant plot / Anna Branford ; illustrated by Elanna Allen. —
p. cm.
Summary: When a creative seven-year-old girl spots a blue china bird that she
desperately wants, she forms an imaginative plan for getting it.
ISBN 978-1-4424-3585-8 (hc) — ISBN 978-1-4424-3586-5 (pbk)
ISBN 978-1-4424-3587-2 (eBook)
[1. Individuality—Fiction. 2. Imagination—Fiction. 3. Moneymaking projects—
Fiction.] I. Allen, Elanna, ill. II. Title.
PZ7.B737384Vg 2012
[Fic]—dc23   2011022584

For Sylvia (my granny)
—A. B.

Garjean, this is for you
—E. A.

1
The Red Button

Violet Mackerel is quite a small girl, but she has a theory.

Her theory is that when you are having a very important and brilliant idea, what generally happens is that you find something small and special on the ground. So whenever you spy a sequin, or a stray bead, or a bit of ribbon, or a button, you should always pick it up and try very hard to remember what you were thinking about at the precise moment when you spied it, and then think about that thing a lot more. That is Violet's theory, which she calls the Theory of Finding Small Things.

"Wake up, Violet," says Violet's mama. "It's nearly five o'clock."

It is Saturday, which is market day. Violet yawns. It is still dark. Mama's hair is a bit damp from her shower and it smells like mangoes and blossoms. Violet leans forward for a snuggle and nearly falls asleep again.

"Just stay awake until we're all in the van," says Mama. "Then you can sleep as much as you like."

Violet's big brother, Dylan, and big sister, Nicola, are already awake, and they are helping to load up the van with fold-up tables and chairs, the big canopy umbrella, and boxes and baskets of Mama's knitting. They are going to the market like they do every Saturday morning, to sell the woolly things Mama makes.

Violet thinks she would quite like to wear her pajama bottoms under her skirt today. They feel nice and warm from bed. Sometimes if you say things like "Can I wear my pajama bottoms to the market?," people say things like "No." But if you just put your skirt on over the top, and have your eyebrows slightly raised like someone who is thinking of something very important and interesting, no one says anything at all.

When Violet, Mama, Nicola, and Dylan arrive at the market, even though it is still not properly light, lots of people are already there, bundled up and rubbing their hands together with coldness, unfolding and unpacking their things to sell. No one notices Violet's pajama bottoms.

Violet's favorite person at the market (apart from Mama and Dylan and Nicola and herself) is a man who never smiles. He sells china birds, small enough to fit in the palm of your hand, and he is there every week. Violet says hello to him as she always does, and he doesn't even look up, which he never does. But after waking up at nearly five o'clock in the morning, Violet doesn't feel much like chatting or smiling either. So she feels that even though he never says hello back, she and the man might share a sort of *understanding*.

The man's china birds are all

different and all very dirty. Dylan says that they are probably brand-new from a factory. He thinks the man has just put dirt on them so that they will look ancient and he can sell them for ten dollars instead of two. But Violet doubts it. She thinks it is much more likely that he is an archaeologist. She suspects that he specializes in digging up ancient china birds.

Violet would quite like to own one of the man's birds in particular. It is made of pale blue china, the color of a robin's egg. It is always right at the back of the table.

And just as she is having that thought, out of the corner of her eye, Violet spies a small red button on the dusty market ground.

2 The Important Idea

Violet picks up the red button.

She puts the button in her pajama pocket, hidden by her skirt. It is a safe and secret place.

Right when I spied that red button, she says to herself, *I was thinking of how much I would like to own that Blue China Bird. So now I know,* thinks Violet, *that it was not just a silly wish but a* very important *idea.*

However, the bird is ten dollars, and Violet does not have ten dollars. Violet does not even have one dollar. Violet thinks.

It is quite nice to hear the noisiness and busyness of the market growing as more and more people start to arrive, but it can be a bit distracting when you are trying to have a brilliant idea. So Violet gets a blanket and a cushion out of the back of the van and makes herself a sort of nest in the backseat. From her nest, Violet can still see what is going on at the market, but she can think more clearly.

Violet's sister, Nicola, has her own plan. She is a teenager and all she wants is a haircut by a person called Mojo who only works at a particular hair salon on Wednesdays. Nicola has made earrings with wire and pliers, and she is arranging them on

the same table as Mama's woolly
things. She is pinning them to a cork-
board with a sign reading HANDMADE
EARRINGS BY NICOLA MACKEREL $2.
Violet likes Nicola's earrings and
she thinks quite a few people will
probably want to buy them.

Violet's brother, Dylan, has his own plan too. He is almost a teenager and all he wants is a camera. He is playing his violin next to Mama's stall with his violin case by his feet, and every few minutes Violet hears the jingle of people throwing coins into it. Dylan only knows three songs, and one of them is a Christmas song, and it won't be Christmas for a very long time. But none of the people at the market seem to mind, and he is getting quite a few coins to save for his camera.

When you only want something ordinary, like a camera or a haircut, you only need an ordinary plan, like playing the violin or making earrings. But if what you want is something really, really important, and if the importance has been proven by your own personal theory, then ordinary plans are no good.

What you need is a *plot*.

A *brilliant* plot.

Fortunately, Mama keeps a note-book in the van and she doesn't mind people plotting in it. Violet reaches over to take the notebook and a pen out of the glove box, and then rearranges her nest so she can rest the notebook on her knees.

This is what she writes:

Then it is just a matter of thinking

what to write next.

3 The Thinking Box

Mama sometimes says that it is quite helpful, when you are trying to solve a difficult problem, to think *outside the box.*

Outside-the-box thinking is how Mama thought of doing knitting when Dad left and she was feeling sad. People made suggestions like "Perhaps you could try jogging in the mornings" and "Why don't you take an evening class?"But those are inside-the-box sorts of ideas, and not much good for people like Mama.

Knitting is different.

The blanket Violet is nesting in was one of the first things Mama ever knitted. She made it especially for Violet—soft and feathery brown—because Violet likes small brown sparrows, and she added some purplish patches because actual violets are purple. It is Violet's favorite blanket.

Knitting makes Mama happy and relaxed, even when the phone is ringing and there is someone at the door, and Dylan is yelling at Nicola, "If you don't get out of the bathroom *now*, I will tell Angus Podmore that you *love* him," and Nicola is nearly crying because she still has conditioner in her hair and she *can't* come out. So Violet thinks that knitting was quite a good idea of Mama's.

Violet decides she might try the trick of thinking outside the box. So she crosses out the part in her notebook where she has written "Actual Plot" and instead she draws a big thinking box.

Actual Plot:

Inside the box she writes ordinary ideas, such as:

a tell mama I need the
Blue China Bird for a
school project

B Ask for it for my
birthday

When the box is full of very ordinary ideas, she writes her interesting ideas outside it. These are things like:

a) Dry 10 corn kernels
in the sun and paint
them with white paint.
Put them under the
pillow and if the
tooth fairy gets tricked
and brings 10 dollars,
buy the Blue China Bird.

b) Go on a tv Game show where you win really big prizes, like fridges, by guessing what the missing letters are in "dr_ss_ng g_wn." (Even though the clue is "something you wear over your pajamas before bed and possibly also for a while in the morning.") Then do a swap with the man for the Blue China Bird.

Violet likes these ideas, especially the ones outside the box, but she feels that she has not yet stumbled upon a *brilliant* plot. These are all only *quite good* plots.

Violet must have been thinking and plotting for a while, and maybe even falling asleep a little bit (which is easy to do if you have made a very comfortable and warm nest), because Mama pokes her head in the van and says, "Are you all right in there?"

"Yes," says Violet. "I'm just doing some plotting."

Violet decides to take a break from plotting because Mama has bought everyone some little pancakes called *poffertjes*. They come in a paper cup with a drizzle of maple syrup and a long, pointy wooden skewer to spike them with. They are one of Violet's favorite things.

Violet sits by the knitting stall with Mama and Nicola and Dylan, and they all spike at their *poffertjes* and get a bit sticky. And just as Violet is thinking about stickiness, and not actually about plotting at all, a funny thing happens. The beginning of a brilliant plot suddenly sprouts in her mind.

When she has finished her last *poffertje*, Violet crawls underneath the table of Mama's knitted things. She is hidden by the tablecloth hanging down, so no one can see what she is doing. Using the pointy wooden skewer from her *poffertjes*, she begins to scratch in the dirt.

The top layer crumbles easily away, so Violet digs some more, scooping the dirt into a little pile beside the growing hole with her hands.

"What are you doing?" asks Mama after a while, peeking under the tablecloth.

"Being an archaeologist,"

says Violet.

A good plot is now settling properly in Violet's mind. If she finds something very precious, like an ancient jewel or a rare dinosaur bone, she will become rich and famous for her discovery. Then she will be able to buy the Blue China Bird. It would be good to find even a very small thing, just to be sure the idea is an important one, but so far there is just more dirt.

Violet scratches and scoops under the table. She doesn't find any ancient jewels or rare dinosaur bones. She takes the red button out of her hidden pajama pocket and buries it a little bit in the dusty dirt. Finding things you have hidden yourself isn't quite as much fun as finding proper treasure, but it is much better than finding nothing.

Soon Mama is ready to pack up the stall, and Nicola is saying that if she hears Dylan's Christmas carol

one more time, she will chop off her own head. Violet has not found any treasure. She hasn't even found anything ordinary, like a paper clip or a bottle top.

Just the red button, over and over again.

But she is not ready to give up just yet.

4 The Mind's Eye

That afternoon when they get home, Violet's mama does her French lesson. She is learning from a set of CDs and a book.

"Red!" says the man on the CD.

"Rooooooge," says Mama.

"Green!" says the man on the CD.

"Vairrrrrr," says Mama, as if she has a hair in her mouth.

Mama has been trying lots of new

things lately. Stuck to the wall in the kitchen is a small piece of paper on which she has written the words "If You Can See It, You Can Be It."

After Dad left, a few of these bits of paper started to appear around the house.

"Is that your theory?" Violet asks.

"Sort of," says Mama.

"What does it mean?" asks Violet.

"I think it means that if you can picture something very clearly in your mind's eye, you can make it happen."

Violet quite likes the idea that her mind has an eye.

"What does your mind's eye see?" Violet asks.

"Well, first I see you and Dylan and Nicola growing up happy and healthy. And then when you are all grown up, I see myself in Paris, speaking French and maybe knitting scarves and leg warmers for a boutique or two," says Mama, squatting down to pick up something.

"What's that?" asks Violet.

"One of Nicola's earrings, I think," says Mama, putting it in her pocket, as Violet has explained the Theory of Finding Small Things to her before.

"If I am not *quite* grown up, can I come with you to Paris?" asks Violet.

"Yes," says Mama.

"And if I *am* properly grown up, I will send you postcards from my archaeological digs."

"I would like that," says Mama.

Violet goes to her room, where she
has taken her notebook of plots. At
the top of the page she writes:

If you can see it,
you can be it.

Then she closes her eyes.

Her mind's eye sees all sorts of things, like herself on a talk show with the caption "Girl archaeologist discovers new dinosaur, to be named *Violetosaurus mackerelus*."

The talk show host says to her, "So, Violet, how did you actually find the bone that led to this incredible discovery?"

"Well, Max," says Violet (since Max seems to be the name her mind's eye has given to the talk show host), "there was a Blue China Bird at the market, and I was thinking outside the box about how I could get it. . . ."

The studio audience says, "Ahhh!," because they think it is a nice sort of wish. But they are also amazed by her cleverness. They are all planning to send her china birds when they get home, so she will end up with hundreds of them. Probably all the talk show hosts will want to interview her after that. She might even be the richest and most famous dinosaur-bone discoverer in the world.

Violet opens her eyes again.

"If I Can See It, I Can Be It," she says to herself.

Then she goes outside into the garden, and the real dig begins.

5 The Archaeological Dig

The wooden skewer from the market was a good tool for digging under the table, but Violet suspects it is not the best tool for an archaeologist. There are proper spades and trowels in the garden shed, which will make her job much easier. There are even some old, soft paintbrushes, perfect for getting the very last of the dirt off precious treasure or old bones. And there might be all kinds of interesting things buried in the garden. Violet hopes there will even be a stray sequin glittering in the grass in the sun, to show her exactly where to dig.

Violet assembles her archaeologist's tool kit, and when it is complete, she scans the garden for a sparkling hint. But there is nothing. So she decides to start right in the middle, where the grass is nice and soft. It looks like just the sort of place a dinosaur bone might be.

Violet digs and digs and digs. Sometimes she hits something hard (which always turns out to be a rock or a pipe, and not an ancient bone). Then she works on making the hole wider instead of deeper.

"If I Can See It, I Can Be It," she says to herself.

As she digs, getting hotter and hotter and tireder and tireder, Violet makes sure she keeps on thinking about the *Violetosaurus mackerelus*. It will probably get in the newspaper, maybe even on the front cover, as well as on Max's talk show. Then, when she is very rich and famous, Violet will buy Mama a whole rainbow of colored wool. She will also buy Dylan a camera and Nicola a haircut by Mojo.

They will all say, "Violet, as well

as being a brilliant plotter you are so generous, always thinking of other people and not of yourself." (Although actually, first of all, she will buy herself the Blue China Bird.)

Suddenly Violet hears a sort of coughing, gasping noise.

She looks up.

It is Nicola, and she doesn't look as though she is thinking of Violet's generosity. In fact, she looks more as if Dylan has been talking to Angus Podmore.

"What . . . are . . . you . . . *doing*?" she asks.

"I'm being an archaeologist," says Violet.

When she looks around her, though, she can see why Nicola's mouth is still a bit open. Their small back garden looks quite different with so much of the grass the wrong way up.

"Archaeologists have to make a *little* bit of mess," says

Violet. "Otherwise, they might never find any treasure at all."

"A little bit of mess?" Nicola gasps. "You've wrecked the garden!"

"I have *not*," says Violet very crossly.

"You have *so*," says Nicola.

"Peabrain!" yells Violet.

"Garden wrecker!" Nicola yells back.

Then Mama comes out to see what all the fuss is about.

6 The Slight Disaster

"Oh, Violet," says Mama, putting both her hands over her mouth and then over her eyes. "What were you *thinking*?"

"I was thinking of a *brilliant plot*," says Violet in the crossest voice she has ever, ever used. Clearly, no one is being at *all* amazed by her generosity.

Somehow the discovery of

Violetosaurus mackerelus, the talk show and the newspaper, the rainbow of wool, the camera, the haircut by Mojo, and even the Blue China Bird seem to swirl and drain away like dirty bathwater.

Violet runs to her room and flops on the bed and howls and howls, and her pillow gets wetter and wetter.

After a little while Mama comes in and sits down on the bed next to her.

"Nicola said you were being an archaeologist again," says Mama.

"Yes," says Violet, into the pillow.

"There isn't any treasure in the back garden," says Mama.

"How do you know?" asks Violet, still into the pillow.

"Your dad and I shoveled that dirt there ourselves when we first bought the house, before you were born."

"Nobody ever tells me *anything*," says Violet, wondering what other important information they have all been keeping a secret.

"Maybe you could have asked before digging up the garden," says Mama.

Then there is more howling, followed by lots of hiccups and a difficult time talking.

Mama's hair still smells a bit like mangoes and blossoms. It is nice, when you are having a slight disaster, to smell something like that.

Violet says, "My mind's eye got it wrong."

"Mine sometimes does that too," says Mama.

"What do you do when your mind's eye gets it wrong?" asks Violet.

Mama thinks.

"Wait a bit and then try something different," she says.

Then Violet gets her notebook, and she and Mama think outside the box together about the garden.

Mama looks out the window where the soft patch of grass was. She says she has always rather wanted a Japanese sort of garden, perhaps with a fishpond and lots of white pebbles. Violet quite likes the idea of a fishpond but she thinks white pebbles might not be very nice to lie on in the sunshine, which is one of the things she likes to do when the weather is warm.

Violet says she likes farm animals and has always rather wanted a farm, perhaps with some chickens, a sheep, and a smallish cow, which would eat all the leftover grass so the holes would not be so noticeable. Mama says she quite likes farm animals too, but not necessarily in her own garden, since keeping a farm is a lot of work, and also the neighbors might complain about all the clucking and mooing.

So in the end they decide to go to the plant nursery and buy a packet of bulbs, since the earth has been freshly turned, and it is actually just the right time of year for planting them. Even though it is getting late by the time they get home, they neaten up the holes in the grass and plant the big, knobbly bulbs in the soft, brown soil.

Violet is still disappointed, of course. It would have been much better to find some treasure or an ancient dinosaur bone, and to have been on a talk show, and best of all for the Blue China Bird to be nesting on the table next to her bed. But even so, she quite likes thinking of daffodils and jonquils starting to grow where the treasure was supposed to be.

7 The Leg Warmer

The next morning Violet feels a bit better about the whole garden incident. Sunday mornings are a warm and peaceful time, since it is usually just Violet and Mama because Nicola has basketball practice and Dylan has chess. Mama sits close to the heater and does knitting and Violet sits nearby, doing a puzzle.

"What's that going to be?" asks Violet, seeing the purple and blue wool weaving together like colors in a sunset.

"A bag," says Mama.

Violet watches Mama knitting. It doesn't look too hard.

The archaeology plot did not work out quite as brilliantly as she had hoped, but Violet has not forgotten the Blue China Bird, and her mind's eye is looking out for some new ideas.

"Can I learn to knit?" asks Violet.

"Of course," says Mama, "when you're a bit older."

"I was thinking more like now," says Violet.

"Knitting is complicated," says Mama.

"I *like* complicated things," says Violet.

Mama has some knitting needles that are quite good for a beginner. While she is finding them, Violet does some more plotting in her notebook. The plotting is mostly a picture of some woolly cats and trousers and smallish trees and other things she might quite like to knit. Then maybe she could have her *own* stall at the market, right next to Mama's, and earn enough money to buy the Blue China Bird. (Also, she might be the first person in the world ever to have actually knitted a small tree, so she might get to be on a talk show after all.)

Mama comes back with the needles and casts on some thick green wool for Violet.

"Now," says Mama. "You put the needle through, loop the wool around, bring the back needle forward, and flick the stitch off. Through, loop, forward, and flick. Through, loop,

forward, and flick."

It turns out that two needles and a ball of thick green wool are quite a lot for two hands to do, even before you start looping and flicking.

Mama fixes up the bit where most of the casting on got cast off.

"Have another try," says Mama. "Through, loop, forward, and flick."

Still it does not quite work.

Through, doesn't look right, turn over, and strange knot.

Try to undo, drop, forget which needle, and get cross.

Mama does not have her look of Sunday morning peacefulness anymore. She has more the look of when the toaster has made the smoke alarm go off and no one can find the car keys and Nicola is saying that she is the only person at her whole entire school who does not have a cell phone.

"Knitting is a difficult thing to learn," says Mama. "That box is full of my mistakes."

Violet puts down the knitting needles and wool and looks in the box. Inside it are some woolly squares with slight holes in them, scarves that are not at all long enough, some socks that stop around the toes, and one short, wide tube with some big, loose patches. It is made of lots of odds and ends of wool, all different colors, with spidery threads hanging from it. Violet quite likes the woolly tube, so she pulls it out of the box.

"What's this?" asks Violet.

"It was going to be a leg warmer," says Mama, "but I dropped a stitch or two, and anyway it is much too loose for a leg."

"Both my legs go in it easily." Violet tries it on. "With arms in too," she says.

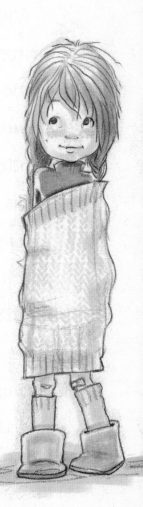

"Exactly," says Mama.

Violet goes up to her room and brings down a box of threads and ribbons and buttons, and sequins, beads, and other things she has spotted while having important ideas.

The first thing she chooses is a green sequin that fell off a bridesmaid's dress. She pushes one of the loose threads of the leg warmer through the middle of the sequin and ties a knot in the end to hold it in place. Then she starts the job of threading something from her box onto every loose end, weaving the dangling threads backward and forward through the knitting until they almost disappear.

While she is sitting on the floor and working on the leg warmer, Violet spots one of the little gold links Nicola uses for her earrings under a chair.

Violet carefully weaves the small thing in with the other treasures.

Even though the leg warmer wasn't exactly part of her plot, perhaps it is part of an important idea anyway.

8 The Tubular Scarf

Every day after school that week, Violet works on the leg warmer. Slowly it gains more colors and dangles, beads and bits and sparkles. On Friday, Violet threads on the red button she found at the market. It

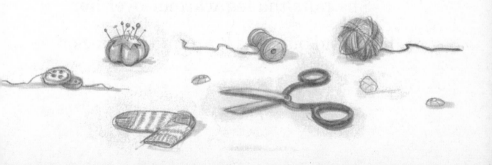

is a bit muddy from being buried and found so many times, but you can still see a lot of the redness. It is a very good final touch.

"Can I put it on the table at the market in the morning?" asks Violet.

"Yes." Mama smiles. "What will you call it?"

Violet thinks.

"It is called a Tubular Scarf," she says. "It works like this."

She puts the leg warmer over her head and bunches it around her neck to show Mama. It fits quite loosely like a scarf.

"Plus, you can do this," says Violet, pulling the back part over her head like a medieval hood.

Violet asks Mama for a shoe box to put the scarf in. But on the Friday night before the market, when the time

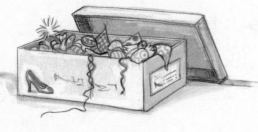

has nearly come to put it inside and shut the lid, Violet finds that she would actually rather keep the lid off.

If someone buys the Tubular Scarf, then maybe she will have enough money to buy the Blue China Bird, which is very important. But Violet wonders if the person who buys it will know it can be both a scarf and a hood. She wonders if they will notice all the small things woven into it, especially the red button. They might not realize that the scarf was made partly by her and partly by Mama. And all those things are actually quite important too.

"Mama, do you ever secretly hope that people don't buy your knitted things, so you can keep them a bit longer?" Violet asks.

"Sometimes I decide I don't want anyone to buy them at all," says Mama, "so I keep them or give them to you or Nicola or Dylan."

"Giving things is different from keeping them *or* selling them," says Violet.

"Sometimes it's nicer," says Mama.

Nicola only needs to sell two pairs of earrings tomorrow and then she will have enough money to visit Mojo on Wednesday.

Dylan needs a bit more for his camera than he will probably get from playing his violin tomorrow, but he is still hopeful.

Violet is sure now that it is all quite easy if what you want is something quite ordinary, like a haircut or a camera. Then you just do ordinary things, like making earrings or playing the violin. But the Blue China Bird is a different sort of thing. That is the problem.

Violet writes on the lid of the shoe box with a purple marker.

TUBULAR SCARF MADE PARTLY BY VIOLET MACKEREL, $10.

Then she puts the scarf in the box. But for quite a long time she leaves the lid off.

9
The Smiling Man

The next morning while it's still dark, Mama says, "Wake up, Violet. It's nearly five o'clock."

Violet decides she will wear her pajama bottoms to the market again, since last week she was especially nice and warm.

Nicola and Dylan help Mama carry things out to the van, and Violet carries the box with the

Tubular Scarf. She keeps the box on her lap all the way to the market.

When they arrive, Violet helps set up the stall.

"I'm not going to put the Tubular Scarf out just yet," she says to Mama. "First I think I will go for a small walk."

Violet walks over to the stall of the man who doesn't smile, so she can look at all the colors of the china birds on his table and check that the Blue China Bird is there.

It is *not*.

The man is busy rummaging in his van, so Violet looks carefully at every bird again, just to make sure. Mama says it is best not to worry until you are quite sure there is something to worry about. But now Violet has checked.

It is *definitely* not there.

"Did somebody buy the Blue China Bird?" asks Violet, who has a very uncomfortable feeling growing in her chest.

The man does not turn around.

"DID SOMEBODY BUY THE BLUE CHINA BIRD?" Violet asks, much more loudly.

"Did you say something?" asks the man who doesn't smile.

And he smiles at Violet!

"Sorry, I am a bit deaf," he says.

"I asked you about the Blue China Bird," says Violet, whose heart is bumping around inside her. "The one that is about the color of a robin's egg."

"Oh, *that* one," he says. "I always unpack that bird last of all, because secretly I hope no one will buy it. It's my favorite."

The man takes the beautiful bird gently out of its scruffy newspaper packaging and puts it on the table. Gradually, Violet's chest goes back to normal.

"It's my favorite too," says Violet. "Did you find it on an especially important archaeological dig?"

"Pardon?" says the man. "You are an archaeologist, aren't you?"

"No," says the man.

"What are you, then?" asks Violet.

He thinks for a bit.

"A backpacker," he says. "I bought my china birds from a potter, who I met when I was backpacking in Spain last year."

Violet thinks how nice gray eyes are with a green sweater, which is what the man has. But he looks as if he needs a

jacket, too. He is rubbing his hands together and blowing on them.

"You look cold," says Violet.

"Backpackers don't mind the cold too much," says the man, whose name turns out to be Vincent.

"The best thing for coldness," Violet tells him, "is to keep your pajama bottoms on under your clothes. Hardly anyone notices."

"Really? I might try that next week," he says.

A thought is coming into Violet's

mind, which is that if smiling Vincent had a Tubular Scarf, he could be nice and warm *this* week.

And just as she is thinking it, she spies a small stray piece of the colored string Vincent uses to put paper tags on his birds. It has blown underneath the table.

Vincent says she can keep it, so Violet picks it up and puts it in her pocket.

Then she goes back to the van and gets out the shoe box with the scarf inside. She finds a pen in the glove box and scribbles out the part on the lid that says $10, but leaves on the part that says TUBULAR SCARF MADE PARTLY BY VIOLET MACKEREL.

She feels a bit shy going back.

"Hello again," says Vincent when he sees her. "What have you got there?"

"It's a Tubular Scarf," says Violet. "I partly made it."

"So I see," says Vincent,

reading the box. "Who made the rest?"

"My mama," says Violet.

"Is she the knitter a few stalls over?" asks Vincent.

"Yes," says Violet, "and she is also a learner of French."

"So am I," says Vincent. "In fact, I plan to go backpacking in France one day."

"Mama too," says Violet. "She sounds like she has a hair in her mouth."

"She *is* doing well, then," says Vincent.

Violet opens the box and holds it out to Vincent. He takes the scarf out very carefully and tries it on. It fits him very snugly, and Violet thinks he looks warmer already. Then she

shows him how you can also pull the back part up over your head like a medieval hood.

"What a good idea," says Vincent. "How much is it?"

"Nothing," says Violet. "It's a present."

Vincent smiles the nicest smile of all.

"I love it," he says. "I especially like the red button."

In a funny way, it is *almost* as good as having the Blue China Bird,

Violet thinks, to see him smiling and feeling warmer.

"Since your mama partly made this, do you think she would mind if I stopped by later on to say thank you?"

"I don't think she would mind," says Violet.

When Vincent does stop by a bit later, he is still wearing

the Tubular Scarf and he puts quite a lot of money in Dylan's violin case.

"Christmas carols are my favorite," he says.

Mama smiles.

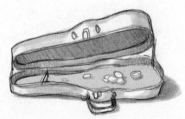

10 The Blue China Bird

Violet is still really only testing out the Theory of Finding Small Things. She is also realizing that no plot, however brilliant, can be absolutely sure to work.

But on Monday, Dylan has enough money to buy his camera, and now he is busy all the time—too busy, even, to say anything to anyone about Angus Podmore when Nicola is taking a very long time in the bathroom. He is always out in the garden, photographing the growing bulbs, which have little green shoots already.

And on Wednesday afternoon not only does Nicola go to see Mojo at the hair salon, but Mama goes too, and they both come home with colored bits and straight bits and funny lengths at the back.

And that evening, while Mama's hair is still special, Vincent comes round to eat a roast dinner and practice French. When he arrives, he is wearing the Tubular Scarf, pulled up at the back like a medieval hood.

They have to turn the volume up on the CD player, as Vincent really is a bit deaf.

"Black!" says the man on the CD.

"Nwaaaaaar," says Mama.

"Nwaaaaaar," says Vincent, who now seems to smile all the time.

After dinner, while Mama and Nicola and Dylan are busy clearing away plates and putting sprinkles on ice cream for dessert, Vincent takes something out of his pocket and gives it to Violet. It is wrapped

in soft purple tissue paper.

"What is it?" asks Violet.

"A present," says Vincent.

Violet carefully unwraps the purple tissue. Then, even more carefully, she unwraps the scruffy newspaper underneath.

And after that, *Violet* smiles the nicest smile of all.

Because there in her hands, sitting

in a soft nest of tissue and newspaper,

is the Blue China Bird.